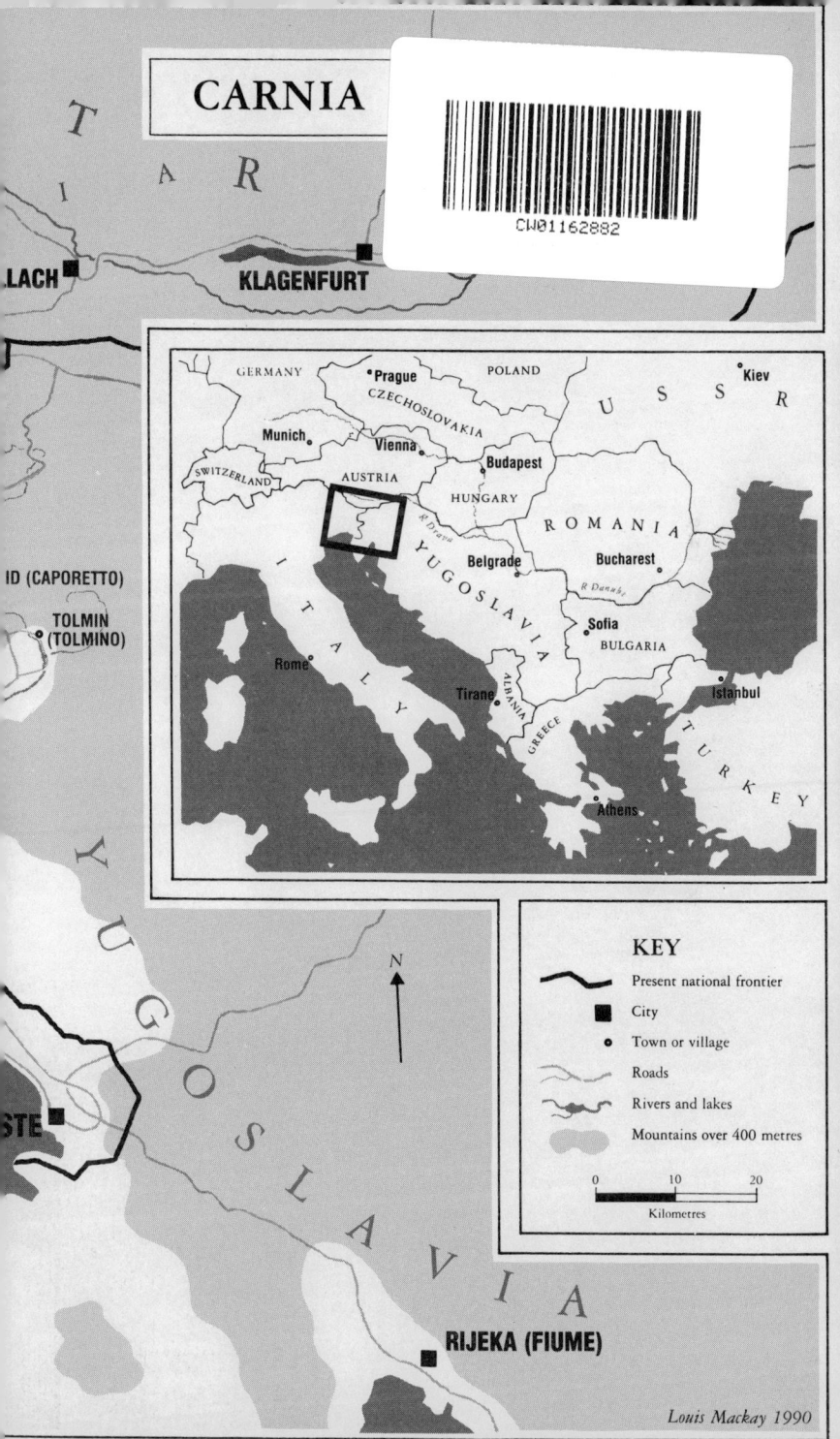

Inferences from a Sabre

By the same author

Danube (Collins Harvill, 1989)

Inferences from a Sabre

Claudio Magris

translated from the Italian
by Mark Thompson

Polygon
EDINBURGH

Original Italian © Garzanti Editore 1986
Translation © Mark Thompson 1990

First published 1990 by
Polygon, 22 George Square, Edinburgh

Set in Bauer Bodoni by Koinonia, Bury,
and printed and bound in Great Britain
by Bell and Bain Limited, Glasgow

A CIP record for this title is available
from the British Library

ISBN 0 7486 6036 4

The publisher acknowledges subsidy from the
Scottish Arts Council towards the publication
of this volume.

Translator's note

My thanks to Giovanna Iannaco, Claudio Magris and Ian Thomson for their help.

MT

My dear Father Mario,

Almost two years have passed since I sent you that report of mine. You asked for it on behalf of our bishop, who was trying, I suppose, to bring some order into the diocesan archives, and wanted an accurate first-hand account of that long-ago mission for the index, and for the sake of any future scholars. It's strange, how close it all seems – or rather, how close it has all been again, for some time now: October '44, Carnia under its improbable occupation by the Germans and their Cossack allies, even the official letter from the then bishop – I believe at the instigation of Father Cioppi, of blessed memory, rector of the Salesian Institute at Tolmezzo – inviting me to go to Carnia with the aim of interceding with the Cossacks, so they might stop their offences and brutality against those unhappy folk. I am still grateful for the kind letter you sent with my lord bishop's very pleasing and too generous reply. In truth I did little enough, but I must confess to accepting his praise with satisfaction. When we are so old, and so many things around us have lost their savour – those long walks on the Carso* are beyond me now, and even

---
* The limestone plateau behind and around Trieste [M.T.]

reading tires me after a bit – we appreciate every little vanity and comfort, and a compliment like a well-heated room.

Those words of yours brought me pleasure and I hoarded them for several months, rather like an old glutton making a box of chocolates last, even though I know very well that after my mission everything continued as before, and that anyway I had no special qualification to succeed in an impossible task. All I had to my credit was my good knowledge of the languages, which allowed me to tell that SS lieutenant (whose name I forget) just what I thought of him, to his face and in good German too, and to stop that old Cossack general on the road at Verzegnis, speaking fluent French at him that was meant, of course, to stir his aristocratic Tzarist soul and dispose it to favour my requests, if only for a few days. All our actions have such brief effects, and afterwards things seem to return straightaway to happening neutrally and by necessity, as if it made no difference to help or harm anyone else, or to be good or unjust. Perhaps we are merely incapable of seeing the consequences of our own actions; at least I can't, but these days I am a pensioner of the spirit.

So for several months I relished those grateful words, as well as the two articles about me in *Vita Nuova*, our diocesan newspaper, with childish *amour propre*. The satisfaction soon passed, but the memories stirred by

Inferences from a Sabre

the report you requested have disturbed something in my life and my memory, which now and then becomes blurred in the tranquillity of my long days. I have been living in this rest-home for the clergy, next to the seminary, for years now – since I became a pensioner, as it were. My room is small but comfortable, I have a few good books, and the meals that the sisters prepare for us would satisfy a palate more demanding than an elderly priest's. The seminary garden is very beautiful, and from up here, on top of the hill of San Vito, I can see the sea, the gulf of Muggia, the outline of the coast. The world these days fits tightly round me, like shrunken clothes; I'm surrounded by limits – including the blue of the sea and the red of certain evenings on the sea's horizon: enchanting limits, which I've loved since I was a boy and love still, and for which I thank the Lord; but limits none the less. And I am weary, I would like to leave, to cross to the other side.

I'm no use for anything nowadays and I couldn't even explain – not to anyone, not even to you – this concrete and serene reality of God, which is all around me. It's not that I am afraid you would try to drag me into argument or spring new proofs on me for the existence of God. Indeed this last expression annoys me: it seems pompous and pedantic. We don't speak of 'the existence of the tree', we simply say – and see, touch, live – the tree, the mountain, the river. And such, for me, is God. But I can't express it, can't make myself understood. I know very well this isn't a matter of some unspeakable mystery inaccessible to reason, as those ineffable and verbose characters claim who delight in every frailty of mind and whom I, Lord forgive me, have always found it difficult to tolerate, because it seemed and still seems to me that they were confusing Christ with the wizard of Naples. If I fail to explain myself, the fault is mine, in my mind or my arteriosclerosis, which becomes more palpable by the day, makes its presence felt ever more. Nor for that matter would I know how to coax from my soul such words as, for instance, 'and clear in the valley the river appears',* even if I feel the clarity of that river with my whole being – and perhaps this is the same thing, I mean the selfsame process.

My days, as I was saying, are long and slow. Time dilates, flows calmly, and often – it seems to me – in circles, returning to shores which it had left behind; and I seem to move in it and with it, but freely, from past into future and from future to past, in a present of everything. It's sometimes as if this mind of mine, which often cannot manage to remember the name of the sister who has been looking after us at the rest-home

---

* 'e chiaro nella valle il fiume appare': a line from the poem 'La Quiete dopo la tempesta', by Giacomo Leopardi (1798–1837). [M.T.]

Inferences from a Sabre

for years, is actually on the point of grasping the secret of free will and its compatibility with the divine intelligence, which knows the future and our actions of tomorrow, so that everything already seems to be decided, including the good and evil that we will do, and we feel that we are slaves, already constrained to be *able* to do tomorrow only what God already *knows* we shall do. So: when I find myself in the past – and in these moments the past 'is', absolutely present and real around me – my deeds stand before me, already complete and irrevocable; but I feel that as I committed them, in the acting of my actions, I was a free and responsible man, able to choose and refuse. And if things already 'are', in the future as in the past, perhaps their future existence does not preclude our freedom. But even as I think I'm reaping this unique and infinite present of events, in which shines our divine freedom to choose, that light goes dim and I am, again, just an old priest who has trouble fitting the key into the lock.

My distractions are few, praying tires me, and as for helping others – the truest religious office – I'm not up to that any longer; helping somebody else means listening to them, following them in their labyrinths without straying from one's own path, supporting them without weakness and correcting them without resentment, identifying with their imaginings without losing touch with one's own, knowing when to turn the other cheek and when to give them a slap, as the case may be. All this is too demanding for me now, and I flee to the comfort of reading or ruminating, which are so much easier than dialogue with other people. I see only three friends, whom I've known for ever, every Saturday afternoon at the Caffè San Marco. I haven't converted them and they haven't converted me, but we play cards, pass comment on the universal story which reaches us through the newspapers, reminisce about our teachers at the high school and the headmaster's nasal voice. Once in a while we'll start discussing the weightiest of matters and exchange a few words with the waiter who brings us our beers (always Franziskus, brewed in Munich). At that table we are at home. If in the not too distant future the Lord should need more information to judge me by, He would do well to turn to these three rather than to the priests who have heard my confession so many times.

But Saturday afternoon is not much; there are so many hours left, the dull hours of a body that no longer desires anything, so I invent pastimes for myself. At first I thought it was just a game with memory: a challenge to its sudden and ever more frequent lapses, a fascinating backdrop for a trick to outwit it. I reread my report, the concision of which you had praised, and tried to add all the details I had dutifully omitted – filling the gaps between the lines or images of my

Inferences from a Sabre

remembrance. I tried to piece together in my head the entire canvas of that tragic and grotesque occupation of Carnia by the Cossacks, who had allied themselves with the Germans and whom the Germans used for the most obnoxious and repellent jobs, deceiving them with impossible promises while inciting them to evil, making them their victims and accomplices, and persecutors of other victims.

The few days of my investigation – which took place, I see from my report, between 27 October and 4 November – gave me an intense impression of the tragedy of those months. Moving around Carnia by motor car and bicycle and on foot, I saw a good deal, and I believe the report caught the essence of it. But the more I reread it and completed it in my mind, the more I felt the need to discover other details, to follow in the tracks of unknown people or even just of names, as if that episode, which touched my life for only nine days, somehow summed up my own truest story, and was the mirror of my existence.

Almost from the start this game – or rather, this affair which began as a game – was condensed into a single image, an obstacle to be overcome. The climax of my investigation had been my meeting with the officer, the one I addressed in French at Verzegnis. In my report I refer to him as 'Colonel', and I need hardly explain that I called him 'General' both from my own hazy knowledge of military ranks, and because I hoped to flatter him with a grander title; anyway, it really was difficult to make out the ranking on his garish and threadbare tunic, which looked as if it had been patched together from different uniforms. I've never really known who it was, nor – till now – have I ever been bothered to know. To tell the truth, my report refers generically to 'Russian anti-communist soldiers', although the people discussed are of very varied origins: Cossacks from the Don, the Terek and the Kuban; Georgians, Armenians, Ossetes, Turkmens, Circassians from Azerbaijan; Nikolai Tolstoy, for instance – yes, that really is his name – claims in his vindictive but scrupulous book *The Victims of Yalta* (as you can see, I keep myself amused with sedulous and pedantic reading) that the Caucasian troops stationed at Paluzza included soldiers from seventeen different language-groups.

The officer heard me out and replied with the bearing of a leader, a commander who can take great decisions, not like someone answerable only for his own unit. It is true that the generals in that scattered, ragged and intrepid army were as numerous as the soldiers, and awarding oneself a pair of epaulettes was as easy as saddling up a stolen horse. And perhaps it is just my own imagination which persuades me that I stopped a warrior on the road, so that I can feel like a mini-Hegel

Inferences from a Sabre

who doesn't merely gaze upon a miniature Napoleon, a little World-Spirit on horseback, but plants himself audaciously before him and bandies words with him. Sometimes it seems to me – or I catch myself trying to convince myself – that it was really him, the commanding officer, Krasnov, the *Atamàn* himself, the White general from the civil war, the author of vivid and compelling *feuilleton* novels, who had come to play and lose the game a second time, among the desolate mountains of Carnia.

Apart from the rank of colonel, my description of him in the report contrasts with Krasnov's appearance; I mention a 'flowing white beard', while a photograph from those months shows Krasnov with white hair cropped very close, and thick, fatherly moustaches, but no beard. I have also read – though of the historians' dubious reliability in this respect, I shall have more to say – that Krasnov would have reached Carnia later, barely by February '45, while the Cossacks had been in occupation since 4 October. Nor am I even so sure any longer about the colonel's flowing beard; I can't say whether I remember it because that's what I really saw or because it's what I wrote: whether the officer comes towards me from the past, from that hour in that street in Verzegnis, or from these lines in my report, here in front of me. I can see a flowing white beard, but perhaps it is only words – letters of the alphabet stamped out by my typewriter – which invented this image. What has happened to me is what happens to those witnesses interrogated by the police, who no longer know if they recognize the photograph because they've seen the face before, or if they recognize the face because they've already seen it in the photographs the police showed them.

So I wanted to know who that colonel-general, so uselessly benign, was. I started by reading some articles and books which discuss those months, by looking out other books which were quoted, or people who, as I later came to know, had witnessed those events. The lending service of the city library, which apart from anything else is close to hand, functions quite well; a former pupil of mine, who has become a suspiciously pedantic manager of the local branch of the National Institute for the History of the Liberation Movement, procures publications and memoirs for me which otherwise moulder in provincial bookcases and archives; and a couple of parish priests in Friuli have helped put me in touch with people who know far more about those months than I could see in nine days.

Except for my breviary, the little library in my room could be mistaken for that of a nostalgic White Russian exile or a humble historian of the resistance. I have browsed through and annotated these epic, fussy or tendentious volumes: *Tragödie an der Drau*, by Josef

Inferences from a Sabre

Mackiewicz; Peter Huxley-Blyth's precise details in *The East Came West*, published in Ohio in 1964; the impassioned memoirs of General Naumenko; M. Šatov's voluminous bibliography; the documentary reconstructions of Mark R. Elliot, published in the *Political Science Quarterly*, 1973, I, xxxviii; Gortani's and Ermacora's scrupulous testimonies; Gervasutti's steadfast and heartbroken book on the life and times of the Osoppo Brigade; and Menis's fluent recollections.

Like all printed paper, these books, whether they are published in New York or in San Daniele del Friuli, are also records of melancholy: the melancholy of lives bent over pages, index cards and bibliographies which will be given away to a bric-a-brac merchant by the next of kin and which wind up, at best, immortalized in a footnote or two. But for me – and I am not much more alive than they are – these papers, where I can find my own pathetic obsession reflected, are company of a sort. There are many letters too, including some from one General Boris J. Varat, who escaped the collective suicide in the Drau, when many Cossacks threw themselves into the river at the very moment that the English treacherously handed them over to the Soviets; a man I will never meet (he lives in Monaco, and my travelling days are over), who doggedly supplies me with precise and for the most part useless information – names, dates, regimental numbers and so forth.

At first I wanted to know if my colonel-general could have been Krasnov – which is unlikely. This pursuit led me to follow in Krasnov's footsteps, reconstructing his movements, retracing or guessing his tracks, as if, by plotting the arc of his rise and fall, I might decipher my own, albeit inside-out. As I tried to complete my little investigation, I felt I was penetrating the strange construction of an enigma – an enigma woven around the death of Krasnov. Every death is a mystery, and for a Christian, death is the decisive moment of life, the moment when its definitive truth is revealed. But the more I read, the more it seemed to me that in Krasnov's case, a second mystery overlies the great mystery that he shares with every man – a much more wretched and vulgar one, but no less revelatory of a secret truth: the riddle (rather cobbled together, what's more, and not even difficult to puzzle out) of false and distracting details which had accumulated around the places and means of his death – as if the mystery of faith was being confounded with the mystery of a crime novel.

Something drew me to investigate the causes and forms of this concealment, which only increased the uncertainty of a period which is already so fragmented. I started, if my memory serves, with an article printed in the *Corriere di Trieste* on 13 August 1957, which that old pupil of mine brought to my attention. It's a feature article about the transfer, a day or two before,

Inferences from a Sabre

of a corpse from the cemetery at Villa Santina, one of those villages in Carnia where life is like a bar in a railwaystation. Three German officers were reported as arriving by motor car and heading straight for the cemetery. The article describes the broiling heat, the boxed-in valley, the white wall of the cemetery, the shadow cast on that wall by the barren mountain side, and the incessant noise of a waterfall. The *Corriere di Trieste*, after all, with its nostalgia for the double-headed eagle and its municipal banner of the Free Territory, was not without literary ambitions, and I remember Umberto Saba* once describing it as the finest newspaper in Europe – probably to snub public opinion in the city, for that daily paper was not so hostile to Marshal Tito, and people hated it.

In this article Bruna Sibille Sizia's pen dwelled with *pietas* and discretion on the details of the 'disinterment operation': the old woman who unlocked the cemetery; the grave with no headstone, marked in the thick grass only by a wooden cross; the grave-digger's spade uprooting the ample vegetation; the rotting coffin

---

* The double-headed Hapsburg eagle was an emblem of the Austrian empire, to which Trieste had belonged until 1918. The Free Territory, or *Territorio libero di Trieste*, (1947–54) was an attempt by the United Nations to resolve the post-war Italo–Yugoslav dispute over Trieste by internationalizing the city and its zone. Umberto Saba (1882–1957) was Trieste's greatest poet and one of Italy's finest. [M.T.]

which emerged from the ground; the Cossack insignias and spurs jumbled with the spectacles, gold teeth and other, more friable remains of the anonymous man who had been buried there twelve years before.

The three officers had been sent by the *Volksbund Deutsche Kriegsgräberfürsorge*, for the purpose of identifying the Cossack general buried at Villa Santina and taking his bones to a cemetery in the vicinity of Lake Garda, where German soldiers and their allies who had fallen in Italy were being gathered. So the three officers hurriedly put what little remained of their old ally into a box – though not, the careful journalist reports, before picking out and pocketing the gold from the teeth and spectacles, just as in the good old days of the war – and went. The grave digger picked up the boots and some shreds of clothing that the Germans had rejected, and the old custodian chatted for a while, reminiscing about the Cossacks who occupied Carnia between October 1944 and May 1945, their combination of brutality and kindness, their destiny as men cheated and sent to the slaughter.

Exhumed and almost pilfered with such casual, undignified haste, the corpse had – and this was the only certain datum – finished under that wooden cross on 2 May 1945, because of a pistol shot in the Val di Gorto near the stream called San Michele, fired at the retreating Cossack column which was trying to escape

Inferences from a Sabre

being surrounded by the partisans and reach Austria. Twelve years are many, but they are also few: strangely enough, they are few for the single individual, whose life is so short, and a lot for history, which spends in centuries. Twelve years ago I moved into this rest-home, and I still haven't changed the shelves in my bedroom for a bigger set, as I've been meaning to do since the first day, because there is always something more urgent to see to, and next week I really could find time to go and buy some new ones. But whereas for an individual twelve years pass like an interval in the bus-shelter, when you've missed your connection and sit there keeping an eye on your bags, twelve years in history is an epoch, full of great events and crucial changes: the entire Third Reich lasted just twelve years, Napoleon's empire scarcely more, and the twenty years between the two world wars seems an age in itself. After twelve years, I thought as I read the article, the general had his funeral rites, a burial and a grave with Christian name and surname, as if the pistol shot on 2 May 1945 had only reached him the day before, and only a few fleeting hours had passed between May 1945 and August 1957, the flickering span between death and burial.

If we take the title of that newspaper article at its word, there appears to be no room for doubt about the name which had finally been conferred upon both the corpse and its grave: 'Three Germans take charge of the bones of Atamàn Pjötr Krasnov'. It seemed, says Bruna Sibille Sizia, a settled matter, 'after which the general's identity was discussed for a long time'; the three German officers clearly must have done something to confirm this identification, or have verified it indirectly, at least. The bones which the men from the *Volksbund Deutsche Kriegsgräberfürsorge* had come to rummage among were, so they claimed, the remains of General Pjötr Krasnov, the *Atamàn* of the Cossacks from the Don, who fought the Bolsheviks in 1918 and afterwards led a nostalgic and colourful life in exile, publishing his lively, picturesque historical novels with some success, before the Nazis plucked him from oblivion to set him at the head – an old man now – of the allied Cossack army, with the promise that they would create a *Kosakenland*, an autonomous Cossack homeland, there among the villages and mountains of Carnia.

'It looked', wrote the journalist reporting the exhumation, 'as if the Germans were playing out another of their tricks to harm the *Atamàn*, their deluded and ingenuous ally'. When a sabre hilt was seen sticking out of the soil loosened by the grave digger as he carried off the remnants unclaimed by the three officers, the journalist had no doubt that it belonged to Krasnov's sabre; it seemed to her the symbol of final surrender, as

Inferences from a Sabre

if expiating the evil which had been done, and at the same time a humble and dignified gift. The *Corriere di Trieste* printed a photograph of this bladeless hilt: brown, curved, finely inlaid, it seems evocative of solitude: promise of glory and mark of vanity, brief illusion of security and support for the hand which, gripping it, had believed itself less alone in the flux of things.

The earth has yielded up the hilt, but not the blade: a weapon which can no longer wound, a standard without a regiment, a horse without a rider. There is something dauntless about the hilt in the photograph – a grandiloquent gesture of defiance, threatening what it could never perform. A false gesture, but made with authentic courage. And the hilt is false too: it didn't belong to Krasnov. According to Pier Arrigo Carnier, a sound if resentful historian, Krasnov drew his own sabre from his belt on 27 May 1945 in Austria, in the valley of the river Drau, and presented it to the English, before the English – to whom the Cossacks had surrendered in the certainty that *they* would never hand them back to the Soviets – delivered him to the Russians, together with his men. Others maintain, more fancifully, that the fleeing Krasnov bartered his weapon with some Carnian highlanders, maybe in exchange for a bit of bread and cheese, which Cossack sabres could no longer plunder from the villages.

Plainly, the general who unbuckled his belt on 27 May in the valley of the Drau had not fallen in the Val di Gorto twenty-five days before, and was not buried at Villa Santina. Yet even in 1961, in a note to pp. 124/5 of his careful study (printed in Udine by the admirable publishing house of Del Bianco), Francesco Vuga could take it for granted – citing in his support the findings of the *Volksbund Deutsche Kriegsgräberfürsorge* committee – that the unknown man killed on 2 May was Krasnov, and deny that it might be Fëdor D'jakonov, a former Tzarist officer turned German collaborator, killed by the partisans.

It's not the truth I am searching for so much as the reasons and explanations. Even in Krasnov's case the truth is one, clear and simple, as it always is. Yea, yea, nay, nay, as the Evangelist says, and that is all. A scruple of precision, an old man's scruple perhaps, even leads me to respect, in my ignorance of course, the correct spelling of Russian names, even if, when I think of the old green covers of his novels in their rough and ready Italian translations, I feel like writing 'Krassnoff'. Ambiguity is an excuse that weak people use to blame the world for their own inability to perceive differences, like someone colour-blind accusing the grass and the poppies of having indistinguishable colours. As early as 1947 – on 12 January, according to Nikolai Tolstoy – the Soviet authorities released the news of Krasnov's

Inferences from a Sabre

execution, hanged in Moscow along with the other Cossack generals Škuro and Domanov, and the German von Pannwitz, who after 1942 had commanded a Cossack division mustered by the Nazis inside Russia. In his 1965 study, Pier Arrigo Carnier quotes *Pravda* of 17 April 1947 as a source pertinent to the death of Krasnov – which occurred, he claims, on 16 January of that year.

Cino Boccazzi, on the other hand, who spent the winter of 1944/45 as a liaison officer in Carnia with the Allies and the partisans, writes in his book *Missione Col di Luna* – and not only in the first, 1957 edition, but also in the more recent one of 1977 – that Krasnov ('small, old, laden with Tzarist crosses and medals', and – though at this point he lets himself get carried away, I suspect, by antipathy or embellishment – 'almost always drunk') fell under partisan fire. He adds, moreover, that a scorched book was found in his motor car – the old Fiat, now riddled with bullet holes, which everyone remembered the *Atamàn* travelling in. The book was one of Krasnov's own novels, *Understanding is Forgiveness* – an elegiac, woolly epic of Cossack liberty stifled, needless to say, by Bolshevism, and a bad book too (for he wrote some quite good ones, with a literary expressiveness and facility which one would not expect from an *Atamàn)*.

As you can see, I pass the time idling through a

bibliography which is fraught with innuendo and evasion. There must be a tenacious illusion in that hilt or in that missing blade, insinuating itself into these denials of reality, wanting to convince us at any price that the dead man at Villa Santina was Krasnov. Even Neris, a conscientious Germanist who comes to look me up every now and then, wrote an article in the *Corriere della Sera* a few years ago in which it is clear to see how his scholarly scruples oblige him, *obtorto collo*, to mention the execution in Moscow, but glancingly, on the wing, as if inviting readers to forget these few sentences with their truthful submission and abandon themselves instead to the game of conjecture: a game which, in the name of a hidden meaning of some sort – in the name, one might once have said, of the truth of art – favours the version that makes Krasnov die in the Val di Gorto and be buried in an unmarked grave, which is later opened up and despoiled.

This laborious and subtle resistance on the part of the falsification almost persuades me to set up as an historian myself, a dilettantish historian who doesn't reconstruct the facts but rather the distortion of the facts. I contacted the parish at Verzegnis, since I knew that Krasnov had often talked to the priest there – and very affably, so they say. He also gave this priest several of his novels and promised him, as he did me – I mean, as my colonel-general promised me – to put a stop to the

Inferences from a Sabre

thievery and violence which sometimes led his men astray, or at least to mitigate it. I don't wonder that my colleague at Verzegnis was hardly more effective than me. Krasnov could do nothing; he was in the grip of the war and its inexorable mechanism, and of the Germans, with whom he actually believed he was dealing on equal terms.

The priest at Verzegnis, Father Caffaro, has since passed to a better life, but his former sacristan, a certain Zorzut – a pupil of the Salesians at Tolmezzo, who trained as a teacher and now keeps himself busy with a course in social studies – remembers those days very well and is, indeed, happy to get the chance to talk about them, so when I tracked him down he didn't wait to be asked before gratifying my curiosity. Krasnov did not – so Zorzut says – receive anybody at his headquarters, which he established in the 'Golden Star' inn at Villa di Verzegnis, except the occasional Russian or Georgian princess, who rolled up from who knows what haunt of exile and greeted him according to the rules of an ancient etiquette. He never agreed to parley with representatives of the partisans or delegations from the populace, because it was inconceivable to him to treat with anyone below his own station, and he thought the partisans – whom he may well never have seen in the flesh – were no better than the dregs which, he was firmly convinced, seep from the lower depths whenever revolutions destroy faith in God, authority, degree, the regiment, duty, and self-sacrifice.

His books, written so many years before, seethe with this hatred and contempt, which perhaps are born of fear and are certainly the sign of a man who has lost his head and is losing his soul, who is no longer capable of seeing his way in a world that changes and who burdens other people with his own anxiety and inadequacy. In *Understanding is Forgiveness* – a book devoid alike of understanding or forgiveness, which one untenable version of the legend discovers beside his corpse in the bullet-riddled Fiat – he describes the Russian Revolution as a disgusting mire, as a sieve which dredged the worst rabble, the riffraff, the scum of the army to the surface and to light. He works himself into a seditious and hyperbolical froth of invective, describing the Reds as imbeciles, layabouts, men rotted by disease, without eyebrows or noses, hospital inmates, invalids left behind to guard the dregs who, thanks to Bolshevism, had resurfaced to vent their spleen.

According to Zorzut, the old *Atamàn* had no dealings with those unknown people fighting in the mountains – fighting bravely and gallantly, as he had to admit – who reminded him of something craven and uncontrolled: of everything that as a young man he thought he had seen in the Bolshevik revolution, and described in his books as filthy red sewage. In his little room at

Inferences from a Sabre

Villa di Verzegnis, now transformed into a princely pavillion of the steppe, he was expecting to negotiate at least with Field Marshal Alexander, who had fought against the Bolsheviks in Courland twenty-five years before, just as Krasnov had; or with Churchill himself, who in his time had also supported and subventioned Denikin's White Army. So he collaborated, like the last foot-slogger, who knows not whither or for whom he marches to his ironic destiny – a destiny which in Krasnov's case lay, so he himself believed, within his grasp, for him to wield as imperiously as if it were his sabre.

Had he agreed terms with the partisans, he might have saved himself and his men; but he insisted on waiting for the English, and it was precisely they who transferred him to the Soviets, under the secret provisions of the Yalta conference. Until the very last, on the eve of the hand-over to the Soviets, he was writing trustingly to Alexander, as an equal, without getting any reply. Krasnov, who claimed to be the *Atamàn* of a nation of knights-errant, did not understand that his equals were those other nomads and vagrants fighting in the mountains to defend their homeland, which he – as champion of the patriotism banished by the 'Red and Jewish international' – had come to occupy and steal, without even realizing he was doing it, on behalf of a third party, as the faithful minister of a savage dispossession.

But from the start he had no intention of dealing with the victors of his own rank, probably because he thought he was the victor himself. He would climb out of his car, Zorzut tells me, with an advance-guard of twenty-four mounted Cossacks and as many again bringing up the rear, all in their blue cloaks and bearing rifles and sabres. He paid meticulous attention to their uniforms: the dark blue cloth, the breeches with the flame-red stripes, the silver-plate buttons on their tunics, the buckles on the horses' harnesses. It was necessary, he said to Father Caffaro in one of their first conversations, to oppose the diabolical disorder unleashed by the revolution with the precision of military life, regulated minute for minute by indisputable rules and commands. But even at the time, Zorzut says, those words sounded muffled and unreal to Father Caffaro, as in a dream, because he seemed to have heard them before. He had recently read one of the books the *Atamàn* had given him, and he realized that Krasnov's words now were the same ones which, in his book, he had put in the mouth of Fëdor Michajlovič, a Tzarist general whom fate and his own too-cunning plan bring to fight in the Red Army, with the secret purpose of helping the Whites. Fëdor Michajlovič becomes trapped in the plot of his own faithlessness, which he expiates in the end with his death. It was Father Caffaro's impression that, while Krasnov believed he was laying down

Inferences from a Sabre

the law to the future, he was following a prompt-book with the words and part of one of his own characters – a character swept away by his own ingenuous conviction that he could take history for a ride, could outsmart the course of events and even control it.

While Krasnov exalted the discipline and order of the uniform, what Zorzut and the other witnesses from those months remember is the ragged and motley confusion of his army – the mismatching liveries, the ill-assorted weapons, the grimy caps, the wagons with families and household chattels, the horses, camels and dromedaries in the snow; a rickety *landau*, with ornaments bundled inside. My friend in Monaco, General Varat, often begs me not to confuse the Cossacks, whom he would have as disciplined and self-possessed, with the Caucasian bazaar quartered at Paluzza – with the Georgians, for example, led by 'Sultan' Keleč Girej, who was suddenly and secretly abandoned one night, a few days before the final catastrophe, by his Nazi officers. This whole incongruous and convoluted episode is nothing but a story of escapes, often disguised as attacks and advances; and maybe this is why I feel so close to it, because, except for rare moments of living in God's grace, in glad harmony with the things around us, the whole of life seems to me to be an escape, a forced and forcible retreat. Zorzut tells me that Krasnov worshipped order, and, whether out of kindness or prudence, Father Caffaro never let him know that although sumptuous carpets had been laid on the first floor of the 'Golden Star', the hearth on the ground floor of that inn, with its wrought andirons, had become a poultry run, with geese and chickens pushing between the orderly officers and visiting princesses.

Sometimes, to thwart potential ambushes or assailants, Krasnov would emerge from the inn suddenly and furtively, without telling his own bodyguards. A few steps took him inside the church and the priest's house; looking up as he crossed the tiny piazza, he could see the sundial on the church wall, with its Latin inscription: *Assiduo labuntur tempora motu*, Time glides unceasingly past. Who knows, perhaps the *Atamàn*, who had perfect French, knew Latin too – like Mazeppa, the Cossack *Atamàn* who allied himself with Charles XII against Peter the Great, and once welcomed that Swedish king with a greeting in the language of Rome.

Krasnov's time passed quickly, more quickly than his rather laboured movements as he climbed the steps to the church. Zorzut remembers one of his favourite gestures: conversing with Father Caffaro, he would face the parapet which overlooked the valley, draw his sabre and point it in different directions, like the sceptre of a shepherd king, or simply like a walking stick. He pointed out places, sketched boundaries, traced hypothetical manoeuvres of attack and defence,

Inferences from a Sabre

fixed imaginary points in that space which he intended to transform into a Cossack homeland. 'That sabre pointing at the horizon', Zorzut writes, with the pathos that he likes to dispense in his letters, 'was an old man's walking stick, but the flash of the blade in the air evoked for a moment the vague yearning glow of certain brief, blustery evenings, of curling sea-waves that seem to shine with the promise of everything we lack. A splendour of transience shone from that blade – a splendour which the *Atamàn*, of course, never betrayed.'

Zorzut says that Krasnov's wife often accompanied him: Princess Lidia, whom he treated with chivalrous devotion and who moved with dignity, but responding generously and with kindness to the women who greeted her, obsequiously and timidly, on the road. 'That pathetic courtesy was laughable,' the former sacristan remarks in one of his letters, anxious to show how clever he is, 'but there was an authentic majesty in those two old people, which not even the absurd extremity of the situation could dispel: the majesty of conjugal affection and fidelity, of a shared life, of a love transmitted in their gestures, habits, and everyday doings.'

Reading Zorzut's recollections, I can almost see the couple together, and I think perhaps that old man was born to end his life some other way, breaking his bread in peace, as the Bible says, beside the woman he had loved in his youth. And instead he arrived here, in our home, to disgrace his own white hair by oppressing people he had never seen, to steal their homeland, which he – yes, he, the patriot legitimist – wanted to transform, by an act of will that the Germans had ordered but that he persisted in alone, into *his* homeland, the Cossack homeland, as though it were possible to change the ground beneath the turf that his horses were trampling, or even to level the mountains of Carnia, if not actually to transform them into the expanse of the steppe. The gesture with which he would pat a little child on the roadside, or protect a peasant from the depredations of his own troops, revealed a spirit which really did know paternal benevolence and love – he didn't frighten us boys, the mayor of Verzegnis has told me – but these little gestures were lost in the tide of wrongs committed by his soldiers and his allies and hence in his name, by the authority vested in the sabre which he brandished, imagining that he gave a signal of command when he was actually presenting arms to the Germans like any sentry at a barracks gate.

The old men at the 'Golden Star' still talk about Krasnov occasionally, says Zorzut, beside the hearth which has not been an improvised poultry run for many years now, and they say the dead man on 2 July was him, and the corpse buried and exhumed at Villa Santina was his. The news of Krasnov's death, an-

Inferences from a Sabre

nounced by the Garibaldi Brigade a few hours after the shooting beside the stream of San Michele, still rings in these old men's ears. Heard directly in those dreadful and violent hours, that news has greater authority for them than any which arrives years later in history books written across the ocean, or after tranquil and patient research in the archives.

It's my impression that Zorzut himself sometimes thinks along the same lines as those old men in the bar, but hasn't the courage to tell me so. And sometimes his silences almost persuade me, as if he himself has somehow solved the mystery of my general or colonel. His mother had a non-commissioned officer staying at their home in Verzegnis – a warrant officer or someone of the sort, he says – an old man with a thick snow-white beard flowing over his chest, who devoted himself above all else to keeping discipline among his men, bawling at them all the time. Zorzut remembers him strolling among them in the evenings, his medals pinned on his greatcoat, among the camels and horses loitering in the snow, lambasting any soldiers he caught robbing or otherwise molesting the peasants. It's ridiculous, if you consider the devastation at Agrons, the killings at Ovaro, the pillaging, the bullets fired in retaliation, but even in a sea of hatred and shame not a drop of honesty and order is spilled in vain. Perhaps the warrant officer who ranted at Cossack women because he found them idle in comparison with Carnian peasant women, was my colonel. And the picture painted by Zorzut's mother merges in my memory's eye with Zorzut's own description of Krasnov, as if they were a single figure, vanished who knows where, because no one knows what became of that crusty 'warrant officer'.

Straight-backed and pomaded – for he perfumed himself lavishly, everyone agrees on that – Krasnov would visit Father Caffaro to praise military order and regulation, and exalt brightly coloured haberdashery above the clandestine drabness of those 'bandits' – as the partisans were called on the German posters – who were the elusive lords of woodland and mountain. But Father Caffaro realized that what Krasnov really wanted to defend was not the symmetry of the army but the picturesque disorder of his own motley troops, whose only true military unity consisted in the individual Cossack, with his horse and the first tunic he could throw across his shoulders. When he set himself against the Bolsheviks in 1917, Krasnov's instinctive hatred was not directed at chaos, as he himself believed, but rather against that order which, he obscurely realized, the revolution wanted to bring into the anarchy of the world; against the law, equality and reason which the red flag wanted to impose on the untamed dust-storm of life.

Inferences from a Sabre

He liked telling Father Caffaro about his life, with solemn gravity and senile reiteration. He talked about his childhood on the Don, about the military mission to Ethiopia in the eighteen-nineties, about his newpaper reports from the Russo-Japanese front, about the Tzarist cavalry corps he led in the First World War, about the Cross of St George awarded him by the Tzar, and of course about the civil war against the Bolsheviks. Then about exile, the years spent in France and Germany, the success of his novels, especially about the best known, *From Imperial Eagle to Red Flag*. A *feuilleton* certainly, a melodramatic nineteenth-century hotchpotch at which Zorzut turned up his nose, but a vigorous and vivacious book too, written by someone who knows how to tell a story, how to animate characters and make them talk, how to keep a firm hold on the threads of a wide-ranging plot. Perhaps, as sometimes happens, the book is more intelligent than its author, who didn't realize quite what he had understood of life, deep down, as he described a face or an evening: something essential which slipped from his pen and that afterwards he didn't know how to acknowledge, or didn't want to.

As the *Atamàn* sat in the priest's house reminiscing about his life, it seemed to Zorzut – who had read the novels Krasnov gave to the priest – that the old man was reading aloud from his own books, and usually the most clumsily written, rhetorical pages. The Ethiopia and Manchuria of his descriptions resembled the exotic *papier maché* lands where the Cossack Igrunka ends up – Igrunka, the hero of *Understanding is Forgiveness*, his worst book, as Zorzut rightly says, a veritable potboiler. In that house, on those evenings, Krasnov seemed no more real than his Igrunka, invented so many years before, who fights in the White ranks but then, as in some television drama serial, becomes a sailor in Constantinople, a seducer of Creole women in Rio de Janeiro, a soldier fighting the Chamamoco indians in the forests of Paraguay.

In the discussions in the 'Golden Star', one or another of the old men always brings up the story of the watch found on the body by the stream, inscribed with the name 'Krasnov'. It is a well-known story, and obviously there is nothing to stop us thinking the *Atamàn* had given a watch to the elderly lieutenant-general, Fëdor D'jakonov – others call him D'jakov – who fell on 2 May and was buried at Villa Santina. It would seem that the Cossacks themselves were the first to spread the false news of Krasnov's death – to trick the partisans and so ease the *Atamàn*'s flight towards Austria. The body was abandoned for the night, then tossed over a wall by persons unknown. The next day some of his soldiers laid it out on a sort of bier and left it in a little shop in Villa Santina, where they held their Orthodox services.

Inferences from a Sabre

At his side lay a sabre, and not only the hilt. It could be that one of his men had broken it, so no one else would take it for himself. In *Everything Passes*, the nomadic epic which is his best book, Krasnov describes many sabres, all of them old because a new sabre, he maintains, has no soul: Persian blades curved like the new moon and so sharp that they can slice a feather pillow tossed in the air; the *volciok* of the highlanders; the heavy Tartar *gurda*; the *frang*, light and sharp as a razor. Kostja, the hero of the novel, is Russian, but he becomes a Cossack when an *Atamàn* – whom he decides to serve in the Turkish war that the Tzar never wanted – gives him a sabre incused with an image of the wolf Ters-Maimun, an archaic animal deity of the steppe. By breaking the blade, perhaps one of his soldiers wanted symbolically to prevent anyone from taking away the sabre of the man who had fallen in Val di Gorto, and so stealing his Cossack soul in the kingdom of the dead. Whereas probably the rust and damp underground had corroded it to the point of separating the hilt, and the blade is still down there, by now a piece of blunt and useless iron.

The witnesses who saw the officer fall on 2 May mention a woman with him, and say that the Cossacks immediately crowded round, shouting that he had killed himself. One peasant remembers seeing a partisan running away, presumably the sniper, while others claim there was a pistol in the mud beside the officer, which could have been drawn either in self-defence or to kill himself. Self-slaughter was not rare among those people in flight, even before the collective suicide in the Drau.

Before she went off with the others, the woman who had come with the old man lingered for a long moment, looking at him with an expression which to some of the valley-dwellers seemed to suggest more than grief. The historiographers and chroniclers of those months don't so much as mention this woman. Professor Donutti, a scrupulous scholar and formerly the treasurer of the Friulan Philological Society, offered me the address of a fellow who might, he thought, be able to give me some information. He offered it, to tell the truth, with an expression of pity, as though to let me understand that he was not pointing out a source fit for a student of history to consult, so much as suggesting a distraction, not very serious but innocent enough, for an old man who in any case cannot put his days to more fruitful use. So I spent a couple of mornings in the Caffè San Marco with one Dr Puchta, an office worker at an import-export company and a fanatical reader of Nietzsche, a left-wing Nietzschean who often recited, loudly and in German, the passage in which the author of *Zarathustra*, already ravaged by illness, proclaims that he is Polish and declares war on the European powers,

40

Inferences from a Sabre

accusing them of oppressing the peoples.

Puchta is one of those exalted and feverish types we usually encounter only in *fin de siècle* literature, a character out of Nietzsche or Ibsen born a century too late, one of those immoralists who thunder against Christian morality and bourgeois conventions and who wouldn't be capable of harming a fly or fooling around with a girl. The world might be a better place if there were more people like them, even if it is a little embarrassing to be there in the café, with people watching, with someone like Puchta, talking in a loud voice, hissing his quotations in German and spitting helplessly in his excitement, while his pale sweaty face becomes covered with reddish blotches. He always carries a satchel stuffed with papers, jottings, books, scraps of paper, notebooks and lists, and he rifles through them, frenetic and worn out at the same time, often furiously losing the thread of his argument.

He had been struck by this story himself and had researched it minutely, with a mixture of muddled pedantry and wild speculation that tends to be typical of these library-vitalists. For the sake of our common interest in the story, he even forgave my being a priest – my belonging to the black tribe that has laid waste the earth and *joie de vivre*. What stimulates him about the story is the all-embracing betrayal that dominates every aspect of it, especially the English treachery, in which he finds, as if distilled, all the hypocrisy of Western-Christian-bourgeois civilization. He has, so he claims – *relata refero* – traced the woman who accompanied the elderly officer on 2 May; he says she married a timber merchant who lives in a village in Carnia – such cases do exist, though they're rare – and that she absolutely does not want to be identified. According to the woman herself, the shot was fired from the pistol of the *essaul* Ivan Razilov, her then husband or partner, a trustworthy man, formerly *aide de camp* to Major General Timofej Ivanovič Domanov, one of the leaders of the Cossack army, who was later hanged in Moscow along with Krasnov, Škuro and von Pannwitz.

As told or invented, certainly altered and blown up by Dr Puchta, the woman's tale is confused and overwrought – a story for a colour supplement. It is no secret that the obscure events of those months enveloped Domanov in even darker shadows: the suspicion of a double betrayal, which is very likely a calumny but which also belongs to the history of those months, because lies are part of life as well – they, too, exist. Evil is not just the absence or want of reality, emptiness and deprivation of God, as some saints have thought; I believe, dear Father Mario, that evil has being and substance, that it 'is', that darkness is not merely the absence of light, a nothingness, a useless vacuum, but that it has density and substance and is active, per-

Inferences from a Sabre

versely but effectively. The Church has been wise to follow Aquinas in this. The lie is quite as real as the truth, it works upon the world, transforms it; it is here before us, we can see it and touch it, a toadstool which is nevertheless just as real as the edible mushrooms with which Sister Domezia now and then, in the autumn, spoils her old guests – for whom greed and idleness are the only temptations left.

Domanov has been smeared twice-over with the insinuation of treachery. It is to Domanov that Major Davies dispatched – to Lienz, on the evening of 27 May – that invitation or rather instruction from the English headquarters, which itself demonstrates the tangible power of the lie. The Cossacks had managed to take refuge in Austria, whence they had descended on Carnia a few months earlier – Carnia, their new homeland, that land which from one October to the following April had been the steppe of the Don. This whole adventure is a backward march towards nothingness: an endless retracing of its own steps, in front of the *papier maché* stage-sets which conceal nothingness. Thus Krasnov left Russia for the West after 1918, and twenty-five years later donned his splendid old uniform, which he had been parading in the Grand Hotels of Berlin and Paris, and returned to the sites of those battles, to wage and lose them anew, and then westwards again from Austria to Carnia, from Carnia to

Austria, and finally back to Russia and the gallows.

The Cossacks had made their way back into Austria with mixed purposes: with the idea of making one last stand, in the grand manner, barricaded in the Alps alongside the Germans in the so-called 'Kaltenbrunner Operation'; in the hope of joining forces with the English against the Red Army advancing from the East; and others with the plan of allying with the English against the Germans. The only fixed point in these vague and contradictory projects was the intention of fleeing the Soviets at any price. In this state of mind, and with these expectations, they put themselves in the hands of the English. On the evening of 27 May, Major Davies advised Domanov that all the Cossack officers must get themselves the next day to a place further east, in the valley of the Drau, to be present at a meeting where Field Marshal Alexander in person would inform them about their future. Instead of the meeting and the appearance of Field Marshal Alexander there was, as we know, the hand-over to the Russians; with the officers out of the way, it was easier, soon afterwards, to finish the operation of transferring the rest of the Cossacks, disoriented and shorn of guidance, with their families in tow.

Butlerov, Domanov's *aide de camp* who brought the message and translated it for him, was immediately suspicious. Domanov accepted the order and executed

Inferences from a Sabre

it, organizing his officers' journey under the escort of the First Kensington regiment, and persuading them not to put up any resistance. There can be no doubt that his neutral efficiency eased the English task of leading him and his men to their deaths. Some of the Cossacks who survived those days and fled into the woods still accuse him today of knowing all about the trap and acquiescing in the hope of saving his own skin. In his book *The Last Secret*, Nicholas Bethell describes how, on the evening of 28 May, Colonel Bryar of the First Kensingtons entrusted Domanov with responsibility for the Cossacks' discipline, ordering him to divide them into small groups and to give them a talk between seven and eight o'clock the following morning, to reassure them. According to Bethell, Domanov replied that he 'would do his best to carry out these instructions'.

These words aren't enough to prove any treachery; besides, the animosity of so many Cossacks towards Domanov might also be explained by the fact that they never forgave him for being a valued officer in the Red Army and distrust his belated conversion, so to speak, to the anti-communist cause. It is more likely, as Butlerov – who escaped capture and is a talkative witness – thinks, that Domanov, bewildered and unsure, could not at the time see beyond the chaos of that day and behaved with stunned automatism, trying only to parry the problems of the moment and to struggle on for another day, another hour. Rebelling against Bryar, that evening, would have meant spreading panic among his men, driving them on with reckless gestures, exposing them to immediate danger. Thanks to his compliance, the night passed quietly in the camp. Perhaps Domanov thought that this in itself was not a little. So acts somebody harried by death and clinging to the hour of peace that he manages to wrest, even if it hastens his own end. The syringe with which the drug addict punctures himself takes years away but gives him a day. Perhaps each of us lives this way.

Domanov, therefore, was the captain of that convoy of trucks bearing the Cossack officers to the consummation of their adventure. Krasnov himself was in one of the trucks; his son, General Semën Krasnov, had to help him aboard. The hundred and twenty-five Caucasians were led by Keleč Girej, who had donned his old Tzarist full-dress uniform and whose expression betrayed the absolute resignation of Islam. I don't believe, as Puchta does, that Domanov was a traitor. Or rather, this entire story is one of treachery and betrayal, in which it is difficult to identify the true traitor. Charged with high treason against their country, the Cossacks had been gulled by German promises and by their *Atamàns* who, like Krasnov, had persuaded them to have faith; but their *Atamàns* had been cheated in their

Inferences from a Sabre

turn, and many of the Germans who had convinced them to act in their own interests, like von Pannwitz, finished up being tricked by their own scheming, which led them astray and trapped them. Even Major Davies, who sent that invitation and feels shame to this day, lied to the Cossacks – not knowing until the very last moment that the orders he had received and passed on were mendacious – and so was himself betrayed. Perhaps evil is exactly this ambiguous exchange of roles, this confusion of objective guilt with the guiltless bewilderment of individuals, this intangible duplicity undermining what is noblest in us and making every sinner above all a victim, a dupe.

Of course, Domanov would not have been so persistently hounded by suspicion without the precedent of the Pavlov affair, which Puchta insists is the key to everything. While the collaborating Cossack army was still in Byelorussia, Pavlov – who was its military commander – was mysteriously killed in an accidental shooting on the night of 17 June 1944, and there were rumours that his chief of staff had had him killed so that he could succeed him in the command, as indeed happened. The woman Puchta tracked down had confirmed this hypothesis; she told him that Pavlov was assassinated by her husband, the *essaul* Ivan Razilov, on Domanov's orders. The woman maintained that only D'jakonov among the officers would have known about the crime, and not even she could claim to know why he had said nothing: whether not to disgrace the Cossack cause, or from complicity with Domanov, or for who knows what other reason.

At the moment when defeat became inevitable Domanov would have realized that if the English were to take them prisoner, his deed would come to light and he would be punished accordingly, rather than getting the power and glory which he and his accomplice had expected from their crime. Not an honourable road into exile, but infamy would await him. So he would have decided to exploit the hurly-burly of retreat to get rid – with the help of his trusty *essaul* – of the inconvenient accomplice or witness.

During the retreat he put Razilov, the *essaul*, and his wife on either side of old D'jakonov, on the pretext of helping him along. To live at someone's side even for a few hours means sharing his life, passing him the bread and the glass, laughing with him, seeing him tired or asleep. Living at D'jakonov's side for those few hours, even as she was spinning the fatal web around him, the Cossack woman could have had that sudden revelation which shows in a flash the closeness of another, his similarity to ourselves, everything that – in a phrase perhaps drained by age-old use – Christianity calls the love of our neighbour. But for her it was too late, and

Inferences from a Sabre

the belated discovery of this kinship could not make her turn back and abandon the plot that she was both weaving around D'jakonov and being snared by herself.

Some revelations, dear Father Mario, come when it is already too late to extricate ourselves from the mesh of trickery which we have woven for our own backs. Actions have a weight and dignity which we never value enough and which, whatever the facile rhetoric of good intentions would have us believe, are not revocable at our pleasure. It is precisely the first steps in evil that we must beware of; once embarked on the path, whichever path it may be, it is hard to turn back – as hard as for the drunkard who deludes himself that when he has emptied the bottle in front of him, the last one for sure, he'll be able to stop. I don't doubt the Lord hears deathbed conversions, but I believe that if by some miracle the dying man is cured, the conversion won't count for much in his subsequent existence against his entire previous life. It is difficult for the lyric incandescence of a moment to overcome the epic continuity of a story. Habit has such power over us; it makes us repeat the same behaviour with unthinking slavishness, whether we talk about stamp-collecting, smoking, or torturing people. If we once lose control of that first step – lose the freedom to contract innocent habits like smoking and not to contract culpable ones like lying or tormenting other people – we are already almost lost. Perhaps that woman did learn to see D'jakonov as a brother, but was no longer able to refrain, and persisted in conniving at her own downfall.

This at least is how I, day-dreaming, interpret her strange, intense gaze at the dead man, which so impressed the bystanders, and the bitter rancour of her accusations against her husband, as if she wanted to burden him with her own guilt. He however, the *essaul*, cannot defend himself: caught by the English, he was one of those who threw themselves into the Drau, some with their entire families, others just with their horse and a sack of stones tied to the saddle. Puchta – to whom I don't mention my theory about the woman's remorse, because the stench of Christianity would be too much for him – agrees that in the confusion of the moment Razilov would pretend to chase a partisan, firing into the bushes in an effort to convince the others that this was the man who had killed D'jakonov. As agreed with Domanov, he would suggest passing off the dead man as Krasnov, persuading the rest that in this way the old *Atamàn*, who was such a prize target for the partisans, would be able to slip past them more easily and seek refuge in Austria. According to this version, Domanov would inform Krasnov himself about this ploy, making him an unwitting accomplice in his plan and – by crediting the fiction of his own death for a

Inferences from a Sabre

couple of days – helping him to hide the crime. Razilov, the zealous executant and set-designer, would leave a broken sabre beside the body, to encourage the hypothesis that this was a first-rank commander whose sabre, tradition decreed, absolutely must not fall into enemy hands. The nameless man's hasty grave-diggers buried him with whatever lay close to hand; which is how the hilt happened to finish underground, without the blade.

But this did not satisfy Puchta and his mania for sensation. People in Villa di Verzegnis, and in the other valleys, still talk about a treasure which the retreating Cossacks would have buried somewhere in the mountains of Carnia. If you discuss that period with the present landlord of the 'Golden Star', it won't be five minutes before he brings up the story of the treasure, while the locals in the bar correct or confirm what he says and interrupt with every sort of particular and variant about possible hiding-places, and about the Cossacks who came back time and again in later years, to search for it in the valleys, and the strange fellow who came from far away and asked the villagers prying questions. Puchta swears that Domanov and D'jakonov would have buried the treasure at Krasnov's orders, in a place known only to the three of them; then, taking it for granted that Krasnov's age and rank would ensure his destruction, Domanov would eliminate D'jakonov so that he would be the only one who knew.

But in any case, even this alleged treachery – which I don't believe – sees only losers and victims, because Domanov mounted the same scaffold as Krasnov. And the mystery of the treasure will remain a tale for the bars of Verzegnis, however much Puchta's imagination races in its ever more arbitrary convolutions. The Krasnov mystery is not only about the old *Atamàn*. It involves his son too, General Semën Krasnov, who was delivered to the Soviets with his father and sent to a labour camp in the north, where he died a few months later; his grave bears no name, as if this were the fate of the Krasnovs: as if no definite records must remain, only the certainty of returning to the earth. It is also the mystery of the *Atamàn*'s nephew, Lieutenant Nikolaj, likewise arrested and condemned to ten years' hard labour in Siberia. He survived, and in 1955, after his release, was allowed to emigrate to Sweden, where – true to the promise he had made to his grandfather – he wrote down his memories of those terrible years.

Soon after the publication of his book (which I read in the German translation, *Verborgenes Russland*), Nikolaj Krasnov died in mysterious circumstances in Buenos Aires, where he had joined his wife Lili, who managed to hide in the Austrian forests in '45. According to Nikolai Tolstoy, General Holmston-Smyslowsky, who saw a good deal of Krasnov in Buenos Aires,

Inferences from a Sabre

thinks that he was assassinated by Soviet secret agents. Dr Puchta, on the other hand, has discovered a more fanciful and clearly more exciting alternative, which he nonchalantly grants a quite unwarranted credibility. Before he drowned himself in the Drau on the first of June, Razilov would have mentioned the hidden treasure to a few of his comrades, without giving away the location. Some of the survivors hoarded their obsession with the treasure for years, through a combination of greed and a conviction that they were entitled to reparations – at least to take back the Cossack gold, buried in that earth which had not had time to become Cossack.

Puchta eavesdropped in the bars, gathering gossip and opinions, getting worked up and exaggerating everything he heard; he talks about Cossacks returning to Verzegnis, about a foreigner with an English surname and slanting eyes who took a room at the 'Golden Star' in 1958 and again in '62, and went on strange expeditions; about freshly-dug holes discovered here and there; about an elderly gentleman with a military bearing who went snooping around Villa Masieri, near Villa Santina, where the bald general, Mikhail Salamakin, once governed the Cossack Officer Cadet School; about the stranger who paid a visit to Father Caffaro, not long before he died. Puchta is never short of compelling and intricate details, which change every time in some nuance or other.

Somebody, Puchta says, must have suspected Krasnov of confiding the secret to his nephew Nikolaj, and tried to make contact with him when he returned from the land of the dead, only to die soon afterwards. What Puchta adds to this is certainly his own invention, a grand finale worthy of his lucubrations. A Cossack, who now lives in Lienz along with other Soviet refugees, apparently told him that two Georgians from the battalion stationed at Comeglians under the command of Prince Zulukidze, and one of the Circassians from the division at Paluzza, who had also survived the débâcle, set off for Buenos Aires, to stay with Nikolaj Krasnov – who had just completed his memoirs – and wring the secret of the hidden treasure out of him. The Cossack in Lienz, Puchta points out, attributed the story to three Caucasians – perhaps out of respect for the Cossacks' own account of the outrages which they were accused of committing in Carnia, and which they always blamed on the Caucasians, contrasting their Asiatic indiscipline and barbarism with their own Russian nobility (except that five minutes later they would be talking about Cossack freedom eternally oppressed by the Russians). Hence the three criminals of this hypothesis were definitely Caucasians.

In Buenos Aires, Nikolaj Krasnov would have refused to reveal the treasure's whereabouts: not because

Inferences from a Sabre

he wanted it for himself, but because – according to this legend – he thought the gold should not be enjoyed but remain hidden, buried in Carnian earth, as if to redeem the grief which the Cossacks had brought to that land, even if they had shared in the grief themselves. Puchta's slapdash version is a porridge of themes too weighty for their pimply narrator – of myths and symbols picked up from his enthusiastic but careless reading: gold returning to the earth, to atone for the wound that had been ripped open when it was buried; a people honouring its debt; a band of horsemen tossing down their obol from the saddle. The three Caucasians wanted to get their hands on that patrimony, and Nikolaj paid with his life for refusing to divulge its hiding place.

Of course I don't believe a word of this hot-headed guesswork. But I'm struck by the fact that an obsessive motif recurs in every aspect and variant of the story: one bumps into it continually, in characters and personalities who enter the scene straight off the pages of a book in which they have already lived and told their lives, and then, like the shadows of real bodies, find themselves going through motions already complete and consigned to memory. On one occasion when he was in Father Caffaro's house, Zorzut told me, Krasnov – meaning the old man, him, the *Atamàn* – suddenly produced a roll of maps. Great and small, of the most varied scope and scale: maps of Europe, Russia and

Byelorussia, the territories of the Don and the Donez, of Carnia and Austria.

These were the maps of his Cossack homeland, or rather of his odyssey in search of a homeland. On these maps, vigorously, like a general planning an offensive, Krasnov traced the lines of a perpetual flight: from Nowogrudok, a hundred *versts* from Minsk, where the Cossacks had settled, in the Kazačistan* installed by the Germans in '44, in the hope of being able to stay for good; and then always farther west and south, across Poland, Germany, Austria, until that last journey into Carnia, from Villach to Tolmezzo, whence Krasnov would soon retrace his steps. The Germans had promised them a homeland, a *Kosakenland*; the war ground slowly on, the situation of the Reich deteriorated, the *Kosakenland* shifted westwards and southwards on the maps of the German high command, and the Cossack people set off towards it with wagons and horses, women and children, weapons and camels, old flags and chattels. Now they were in Carnia, at the destination which they believed would be their last – as indeed it was, but in a very different sense – in those villages transformed into *Stanice* on the Don and rebaptized with Cossack names.

'When he started tracing the real lines of the retreats

A *Kazačistan* was a settlement for collaborating Cossacks established by the Germans. [M. T.]

Inferences from a Sabre

he had beaten, and the imaginary lines of the advances he had planned,' Father Caffaro told Zorzut, 'I felt yet again that I had witnessed this scene before. And as I watched it, in my mind's eye, grafting itself on to the actual scene here before me, I realized that I was dramatizing a passage I had read – yes, one of Krasnov's own pages, in *From Imperial Eagle to Red Flag*, where he describes Kornilov, the White general in the civil war, examining the map of Russia and the strategic plans against the Bolsheviks, by candlelight in a Cossack hut. Just as I saw Krasnov before me now, dauntless, deluded and obtuse, so he in memory had seen Kornilov, with his drooping moustaches and Mongol eyes, poring over the map.' Father Caffaro fetched the book and began to read, in a voice which strove for irony but was in truth distressed: '"Open before him," Krasnov had written, "he saw the high gates through which the Asiatic nations had passed to invade Europe in the age of Jenghiz Khan and Tamburlaine. Remembering the days of his youth, he could see once more the deserts and peaks of ardent Semiretche, the city in Tashkent pervaded by a poetic melancholy, Fergana, that earthly paradise, and India, a fantastical thousand-coloured dream. How well he knew those regions, ever since his childhood! He hoped to establish contact with the English and open a new front with them, extending to the Urals and the Volga...".'

When Krasnov wrote that page, Father Caffaro went on, he knew that Kornilov's dream, which he had once shared, was bankrupt. Now, instead, he too was hoping to make contact with the English, and was himself becoming the protagonist in a story which he had already lived, told and understood, but which he now forgot – wanted to forget – that he had ever understood. As he planned vague and glorious strategies, like his Kornilov, his own soldiers were being used by the Nazis for little auxiliary operations and hateful persecution, skirmishes, raids and confiscations, compelled to stand guard over the ruins of villages like Attimis, which had been razed by the Germans and the Fascists.

I went to see the remains of the burned houses in Attimis, one icy, clear winter's day, accompanied by a taciturn young woman who had once played in those rooms as a child. Now they stand indecently exposed, torn open and violated, among the tottering ruins. As I looked at them, listening to the woman's succinct memories as she mentioned one or two details of her wartime childhood, I was thinking that every house is a familiar space patiently carved out of the universal void, and that the Cossacks reached that corner of the world to build themselves a house and to take shelter from the indeterminacy of nothingness, and instead they destroyed the hospitable order enclosed by these walls and delivered it back to formlessness.

Inferences from a Sabre

And hearing the words of my colleague from Verzegnis, reported by Zorzut so many years later, I too have the impression that Krasnov is here in front of me, poring over those maps; I don't know if it is really him I see or a character from one of his novels, or even my kindly colonel-general, but whichever, it is certainly a shadow, a papery creature, though no less distressing for that – an actor playing a grotesque yet painful rôle. Without knowing it, Krasnov himself had passed judgment on the extreme exaggerated deeds of his old age when, decades earlier, he wrote in his most recent novel that men in their pride believe everything depends on them, even though, when all's said and done, they are compelled to acknowledge that the great dimensions of history escape their will and are directed by an intelligence alien to our understanding.

Heedless of his own words, he now persuaded himself that everything depended on him – on the will, wisdom and courage of an *Atamàn*. Had he not, as if foretelling his own involuntary, papery fate, quoted himself in his own most celebrated novel, and introduced himself – as one character among others – in the part which he really had played, in 1918, during the civil war? Now, no longer an author freely creating but a novelish figure blindly obeying the plot of an author whose existence he didn't even suspect, he recreated his rôle: a ham actor of his own defeat and captain of his own captivity. The champion of Cossack freedom, he was yet unable to imagine what the fate of his people would be if Nazism were victorious, and he proudly accepted the Germans' permission to adorn the busbies of his favourite divisions with Hitler's eagle.

I wonder why and how he could have been so blind, and perhaps this is why I see my own reflection in him, why I see him as a portrait of every man who at some moment in his life wants to shut his eyes to the real truth and stages an elaborate diversion to keep it out of sight. I wonder what he thought of Škuro, for instance, the general he had plucked from White exile and who finished up on the scaffold with him. Andrej Grigor'evič Skuro, who installed his staff at Tolmezzo, seemed a Cossack chieftain from the age of Sten'ka Razin or Jermak, to which Krasnov had paid monumental tribute with *Everything Passes*: one of those half-soldier, half-bandit cavaliers, protecting Holy Russia against the Tartars one moment, and raiding Russian land at the Tartars' side the next. General Williamson remembers him during the civil war, in the headquarters he had fixed up in a railway carriage, with a wolfskin cap and a guard of Caucasian mountaineers as wild and fierce as himself.

He was an outlaw, sottish and dissolute; once he plundered a big hotel in Rostov with his officers, during a ball. But he was fearless too, and indefatigable, and

Inferences from a Sabre

his singing voice, they say, was deep and thrilling; even in prison, after the Soviets had captured him – and would, as he well knew, certainly put him to death – he told comic stories and defiant tales from the civil war, to uproarious laughter which infected even his jailers and interrogators. The English, who had once awarded him the Order of the British Empire for valour in the 1918/19 war against the Bolsheviks (a war which they put him up to), handed him back to the Soviets twenty-five years later so that they could string him up. He was a sinner, but I believe his courage allowed him to smile at the irony of his fate.

In exile, apart from getting drunk in the bars of Belgrade and Monaco, Škuro earned a living in a circus, showing off his horsemanship in a Cossack costume. This is another story which Krasnov had already written by the time he came to reclaim Škuro: in *Understanding is Forgiveness*, General Fëdor Michajlovič Kuskov, a White exile in Berlin, takes himself off to the Busch Zirkus one night, where, among the trained elephants and the clowns slapping each others' faces, he sees a troupe of old Tzarist officers in Cossack dress run into the ring and begin performing acrobatics and singing the ballad of Sten'ka Razin, the legendary Cossack hero of yore, the scourge of the Volga.

In the novel, Fëdor Michajlovič's heart grieved for them – as Krasnov's own heart must have grieved when, as an exile in Berlin, he saw his old brothers-in-arms reduced to folklorish entertainers. Now he was taking Škuro out of the circus, without realizing that he was joining a circus himself, that he was obeying the production of an *intermezzo*. 'History repeats itself, Lieutenant Krasnov!' says one of the characters in *Understanding is Forgiveness*; but now Krasnov was deaf to his own far-off words, convinced as he was of living a free and proud adventure.

He could not understand the irony of history because he himself was an aspect of that irony. For all his ostentatious and undoubtedly sincere religious piety, he sinned against faith, for above all faith is irony, a grateful and affectionate sense of our own finitude, a consciousness of infinity which sets every boast in perspective. Now he had a company of actors right at his side, lodging at an inn at Chiaicis. Now and then, in the evening, they would stage some vivid and sentimental playlet for him – nostalgia and at the same time a caricature of nostalgia for Old Russia; and he would watch, be moved, applaud, both spectator and actor of the melodrama, rather like those grand dukes who are hired as braided commissionaires by Grand Hotels. He was fighting for his people's freedom – the freedom of the far-off steppe which was present in their every gesture, as he had written in *Everything Passes* – and in the name of this struggle he had founded a 'National

Inferences from a Sabre

Cossack Party' in Prague, which declared Hitler to be the 'supreme dictator of the Cossack nation', even as the Führer, in a contemptuous reference to collaborators, was saying that 'only Germans can bear arms, certainly not Slavs or Czechs, Ukrainians or Cossacks'.

Krasnov must have lost his most elementary taste as a writer when, even before being thrust into Carnia, he dreamed of a state for his people between central Ukraine and the Samara river, which would be called 'Kosakia', like an operetta. What I, an old priest, see in Krasnov above everything else is a sincere but perverted passion for freedom, which led him into mechanical servitude, as is the way with sin. Which is why I see him as one of us, one of us sinners for whom we say the Hail Mary.

Father Caffaro too was fascinated by this distorted love of adventure, which led Krasnov to relive his fantasies. The *Atamàn* was not above talking politics with the hospitable priest, and, on the pretext of doing the priest's housework, Zorzut would stay to hear his confused, dogmatic, rambling and monotonous speeches. Krasnov liked to say that he was fighting for order, hierarchy and tradition, which were all threatened by the revolutionary chaos depicted with such loathing in his books. In truth, as I have already said, he hated the order of the law and the state. *Everything Passes* is a song of praise and farewell to the rebellious, free-roving Cossack spirit: it celebrates the quick and fleeting victories of the horsemen; the rootless nomads' stark and ephemeral homes; the impulse which fades away and is lost; the particularism of the Don, which bridles at every order, even from the Tzar. The 'ineffable scent of liberty on the steppe', so precious to the *Atamàn*, was the liberty of the individual who carries his homeland and his state in his tent, who acknowledges only the horse beneath and the Lord above him, and if he wants to be off, needs only – as the Cossack saying has it – to tighten his belt.

Krasnov saw the revolution as the anonymous assault of modernity, the sunset of the individual, the end of adventure. This equation is repeated in his books to the point of obsession: Cossack honour is always rebellion and violation of each and every order, even that of the Tzar, whose banner flutters as huge and bright as the sky itself. In *Everything Passes*, the Cossacks capture Azov for the Tzar, but against his will and his interdiction; their honour lies in disobeying him and their pride in not depending on him – in being people who had never kissed the cross for the Muscovite Tzar. They aren't loved in Moscow, one of them boasts, but kept at a distance like mangy dogs, because they don't know how to submit 'to slavery, to taxes, to external compulsion'; in one scene in the book, the *Atamàn* Osip Petrovič denounces with bitter pride the hatred that the

Inferences from a Sabre

princes, boyars and bureaucrats of Muscovy bear towards the Cossacks, who are free from excise and work, and neither sow nor reap.

The melancholy of *Everything Passes* is the melancholy of Cossacks rendering their lands and power unto the Tzar, who breaks their freedom for ever; for it was the advent of the Romanovs, described in that novel, which ended the centuries-old autonomy of the horsemen of the steppes, and transformed them into statesubjects. Krasnov, who fought to save the Romanovs' throne from the revolution, wanted to protect or restore the very Cossack liberty which the Romanovs themselves – the modern Russian state – had destroyed, not the revolution. *From Imperial Eagle to Red Flag* exalts Kornilov, the general who fights for the Tzarist cause against the Reds, but also the Cossacks from the Kuban, who, even if they fight to the death against the Bolsheviks, won't readily submit to Kornilov, who is organizing the White Army.

Krasnov's freedom was the savage democracy of the *Saporoghi*, the assembly of the wandering Cossack army which, in the sixteenth century, sat at Sitsch, in the fortress on the island of Chortiza in the Dnepr river. When his novels describe the chaotic councils of war in which everyone decides for himself, Krasnov is always thinking of the scourges of steppe and river, who know no ties and bow to no man, who elect their *Atamàns* at rowdy and uproarious reunions and follow them in acts of reckless banditry, such as those of Dmitrij Višneveckij, which endured for centuries in folk songs. Treachery – which was to carry Krasnov to the hangman's noose – does not exist in that world, because everything happens only in the present and the only loyalty is to yourself, to your own passion, to the comrade fighting at your side, to the banner of the clan and not to any far-off crown, not even the crown of the Tzar – whose medals Krasnov wore on his breast, nonetheless, to the very end.

Many of the Cossacks who had fought with him against the Reds in 1918 had been on Lenin's side in 1917, and in 1919 founded a sort of autonomous state which was meant to be a 'Soviet without Communists' and whose army caps were a symbolic white-and-red; they often changed sides according to the situation, going to fight wherever it seemed they could best defend their own lawless existence. The Cossacks celebrated in Krasnov's novels, who vow on one page that they will die for the Tzar and boast on the next that they are no servants of Moscow, are not so different. When he describes them, Krasnov is thinking of Jermak, the brigand who conquered Siberia and gave it away to Ivan the Terrible; or of Sten'ka Razin, the eagle of the Don, the rebel who leads the peasants' revolt, who plunders and destroys until he is put to death in

Inferences from a Sabre

Moscow on 6 June 1671 by order of the Tzar.

The Cossack is the champion and the outlaw, he is Holy Russia's protector against the Tartars but he's the Tartar as well; as early as the fifteenth century, writes the erudite Klaus J. Gröper, the word 'Cossack' – which originally meant 'sentry' – signified 'Tartar', even though the Cossacks were soon to become the Tartars' legendary foes, despite sharing many of their customs; Daškovič , who fought the Crimean Tartars in the service of the Great Prince of Moscow, liked to plunder Moscow himself from time to time, in league with the Tartars. I sometimes think that those savage and insensate struggles of each against all are a truthful portrait of the senselessness of all wars, which are always fratricidal and treacherous, always self-inflicted violence.

Krasnov's war was, in its histrionics, a war of the sword against the plough – the plough that triumphs in the end and tills the soil whence the swords emerge in rusty fragments, like the putative *Atamàn*'s sabre. That war was the flight of the sword before the plough, which follows the sword and masters the ground that it has soaked with blood and briefly conquered. The Siberian deserts which the Cossacks cross in *Everything Passes* will belong not to them, but to the slow and methodical power of the clerks who follow in their wake.

According to Father Caffaro, Krasnov was obsessed

by the end of adventure, and the whole of Cossack history unrolled before him like a parable of this end, in which he did not want to believe, continuing to flee before the pursuing army of bureaucrats, taxation and schools. 'He was a mediaeval man, untamed and feudal,' Father Caffaro declared, or so Zorzut claims, 'who hated history, modernity, time itself – hated them with all his might, hating them as we can hate the irresistibility of life when it turns against us.' I too believe that he did not have – but who among us does? – the serene humility to acknowledge that his time was past. He must have sensed an invisible enemy nearby, and in his fury he needed to give him a face, so he could slash at him with his sabre.

Krasnov had created that face himself during the revolution, and for the rest of his life he raged against the mask which his own anxiety had grafted onto the flow of history. To judge by the bilious portrait which Krasnov sketches in his novel, Trotsky's worst fault would seem to be that he didn't know how to ride a horse properly, like all Jews, like all new men – those spiders, as Krasnov thought, spinning the web of mediations which in our world binds the individual in a mesh of abstract relations. Whereas Christian love also means the capacity to recognize people's particular features through the anonymous threads of this mesh, and to know that the mesh, sticky though it may be, is

Inferences from a Sabre

no worse than the idols which, in the past, hid the face of man.

Hence there is a stringent logic in the fact that Krasnov threw himself into the arms of fascism, because fascism is above all this inability to discern the poetry in the hard and good prose of everyday, this quest for a false poetry, exaggerated and overwrought. But the logic is grotesque, because Krasnov sought to defend adventure, the horseman and tradition through Nazism itself, the deadliest enemy of tradition and adventure, the totalitarian and technological bee-hive which levels life into a uniformity much more rigid than that imputed to the democracies he despised. By placing his sabre at the service of the Third Reich, Krasnov turned it on himself, against his horsemen and those ineffable horizons of the steppe.

He did not want to understand that he was the pawn in a game which was controlled in its every last move. When he planned 'Kosakia', he was obeying the plans of Rosenberg, who had proposed the dismemberment of Russia into a myriad little states and ethnic regions. He would not accept relativism and therefore he railed against the absolute, to which we are faithful only if we are able to acknowledge it in its limitations, according to our earthly condition, and if we respect those limitations. The Cossacks who were assimilated to the German ranks were treated as inferior beings – von Pannwitz had to intervene personally to curb their maltreatment at Nazi hands – whilst at the same time Krasnov was trying to convince Berlin that recent ethnological discoveries proved the Cossacks were descended from a nordic race, and were of ancient Teutonic stock.

Perhaps, as Father Caffaro thought, Krasnov could see all this yet did not want to see it. 'He was the prisoner of a compulsory ritual,' the priest of Verzegnis told Zorzut years later, when they were talking about Krasnov, as they often did, 'and he could do nothing but react.' Probably 'reactionary' means just this: feeling compelled to react, and not knowing how to act freely. His resistance to history still seems to me like an aspiration, because it faced total defeat and was truly heroic in its fidelity to a beloved and extinct tradition; but these virtues were twisted into an anachronistic and artificial gesture, as if covered and effaced by a layer of grease-paint.

Perhaps every kind of reaction needs this magniloquent pathos, overshadowing human reason, to stifle its anxiety. There is something grand in Krasnov's *no* to mutability; but, locked in a crooked posture, the grandeur stiffens and becomes a caricature of itself. Even if Krasnov's books did overflow with hatred for the Reds, they weren't blind: General Sablin, the hero of *From Imperial Eagle to Red Flag*, who ends up being tortured and murdered by the Bolsheviks, can see the

Inferences from a Sabre

corruption of the aristocracy, the rottenness of old Holy Russia, the injustice wrought on soldiers and poor people, the decay of Tzarism, the barbarity of the pogroms, the atrocities perpetrated by the Whites as well. Now, however, after throwing himself body and soul into the abyss which he flattered himself he had freely chosen, Krasnov did not want to understand anything any longer.

Timidly, hoping to appeal to his cult of physical courage, the priest would sometimes mention the partisans, who really had chosen to live their adventure, because they were fighting for liberty; he talked about the swooping and implacable commanders of the Osoppo and Garibaldi partisan brigades – Ferruccio, Bolla, Nembo, Furore, Gracco, Grifo and the others, whose courage and defiance of brute force at times corrupted even them, unforgivably, into hatred and brutality, to the point of fratricidal treachery, as in the unspeakable slaughter at Malga Porzus. Or, counting on stirring his imagination, the priest would cautiously allude to Mirko and Katia, the fearsome Yugoslav and his lover – the terror and hope of the valleys, who had quarrelled with the other partisans and been killed by them in the mountains, on Monte Veltri, with blasts of machine-gun fire. Preserved intact by the snow, Katia's body had been discovered in the late spring thaw, very beautiful and bronzed, as if she had died the day before. Krasnov, though, had no time any longer for true stories, but only for his own monologue, which he repeated to himself over and over.

'It was the very model of a tragic aberration which we see all too often,' Father Caffaro said, 'which is to say, a good man doing evil.' I understand what he meant. As I have already said, the delicacy – reported by many people – with which Krasnov took his wife's arm in his, or spoke to peasants and children on the road, revealed a man who knew what love, what respect for every human creature, were. And instead he brandished his sabre to create a world where love and respect would have had no place, and where he himself, if his sabre had not already been broken, would probably have been among the first victims.

Beneath his vaunted aristocratic refinement, an elementary – I would even say, a primitive – process was underway. He instinctively treated a highlander with his firewood as an equal, and would have treated any one of them the same way; but his compulsive hatred of ideologies made him a prisoner of the most abstract ideology of all, which he mistook for immediate reality, and prevented him from thinking and feeling in the plural. If one or another or a third highlander became highlanders, he could no longer remember that they were one, two or three of those men whom he knew how to treat with courtesy, and felt

Inferences from a Sabre

instead an obscure threat, a claim, his pursuit by a multitude of 'others' who seemed to want to drag him off his horse. So he felt he had to defend himself – felt the urge to slash about him with his sabre.

In one of his novels he had portrayed an old Jewish woman, who appeared as a sacred symbol of the suffering of the world; whereas for Krasnov himself the Jews were poisonous snakes, guilty of universal conspiracies and plots, contaminators of reality. He would have been horrified to be told that he, through his own actions and choices, was behaving like the butchers in a pogrom – like the murderers of that old Jewess. Something similar, I think, has happened to other famous people, including much more intelligent ones than him, and they too not without nobility of soul. In my younger days, you'll recall, I used to read Hamsun a lot, and I revered him too, as for that matter many of our generation did. Well, I believe that Hamsun was swept to his nemesis – to fascism – by a process not much less primitive and wretched. Whether or not we are good at heart, we are always cruel when we cannot be far-sighted and think in the plural: when, like the apostle Thomas, we only know that a creature exists by seeing and touching, and we don't succeed in truly realizing that there are other creatures as well, creatures of flesh and blood whom we never see but who are as real as ourselves and those we try and help.

So often we are only capable of taking the commandment to love our neighbour literally, all too literally, and recognizing as our neighbour only whoever is materially, physically, animally close to us, we abandon the ones we can't see to languish in their hell. Once, in a novel, the truth that all are equal in God's sight had slipped even from Krasnov's pen: everyone – the Tzar and the shepherd, the Christian and the heathen who worships idols. But this truth could not help him; if we are to save ourselves, it's not enough to grasp this truth just once – we must understand it always, at every moment, and feel it with our whole being. 'And Krasnov,' as Father Caffaro said, 'didn't understand anything any more: he only felt something stormy and incomprehensible, which he, with his vainly eloquent gestures, tried to dress in a semblance of dignity.'

That he could no longer grasp his own situation – or did not want to – appears from a different testimony, which I obtained after many vicissitudes. With some difficulty I managed to trace one of the three German officers who arrived at Villa Santina in August 1957, to exhume the nameless corpse. I wanted to know what their opinion was, if they were aware of any other factor, if they believed at the time that those meagre remains were Krasnov's. My questions were not answered by his polite and unsatisfactory reply, which merely informed me that the remains had been buried

Inferences from a Sabre

at Costermano di Verona anonymously, in grave no. 527 of Cemetery 1. My vague and courteous informant added, however, that I might be able to learn more from an ex-officer of his regiment, one Major von Wojka, whose address he enclosed.

Von Wojka replied straightaway, we exchanged further letters, and our correspondence is perhaps the last encounter of my life, a dialogue which is intense and at the same time diffident, almost evasive. He tells me a lot of things, always about the war and those years, as if he wants to open his heart, to confess, but in a distant, controlled, almost bureaucratic tone, which prevents any outburst. It's as if he were pursued by a hazy and obscure remorse which he cannot bring to definition, so he banishes it, haughtily, to the swarm of emotions and anxieties which brood inside us like darkness.

Von Wojka is the German officer who, in the last days of April '45 – just before the Nazi surrender – accompanied General Vlasov when he flew from Berlin to Campoformido, for that meeting with Krasnov which has been veiled in uncertainty for so long.

Krasnov hated and despised Vlasov because he sensed that this man was his mirror, a truthful mirror reflecting the void – a mirror you look into and see nothing. And he hated him because he was the supreme commander of the ROA, the *Russkaja Osvoboditel'naja*

Armija of Russian collaborators, organized by the Germans and mustered from the ranks of the Red Army. Andrej Andreevič Vlasov was a Red Army general, a Russian patriot and military genius who defended Kiev and Moscow brilliantly against the Nazis, and even scored lightning defeats on them from Moscow. A loyal patriot and military man, he had witnessed the Stalinist terror at the time of the great purges, decimating the highest echelons of the army around him, eliminating many of his friends and fellow soldiers; since that time he had been dreaming of a united and independent Russia, free from the tyranny and social injustice which he had fought against ever since enrolling in the Bolshevik ranks as a very young man.

When the Germans, who had taken him prisoner in 1942, gave him the chance to form an alliance and lead a Russian army against the Soviets, this clear-headed and taciturn general was probably dazzled, just for a moment, by one of those temptations which almost always carry a man to perdition, when he thinks he is more astute than other men and capable of bending destiny to his own Machiavellian ends. Vlasov had none of Krasnov's feudal nostalgia: he could see the Nazis slaughtering his people and the contempt with which they treated even their Russian allies. He had no illusions about Hitler's friendship, but he succumbed to

Inferences from a Sabre

a more dangerous illusion, that of being able to manipulate events. Probably convinced that the Reich would win, he sought a better fate for his country, in the future world dominated by Nazism. With German help, he thought, he could defeat Stalin and build a Russian army at the same time – one strong enough to protect a new, free Russia against the Germans, who were hardened by battle on so many fronts.

He too was confident at first that he could use the Germans, who were toying with him. 'In Berlin only Rosenberg took him seriously,' von Wojka wrote to me, 'but even the Nazi inner circles thought that Rosenberg and his *Myth of the Twentieth Century* were idiotic. Rosenberg proposed to split Russia into a great number of little ethno-political units, so he encouraged Krasnov, even as he feared the new united Russia of Vlasov's dreams. But everyone knew that *that* Russia would never exist.

'Headquarters appointed me to Vlasov's general staff, as a liaison officer. Vlasov realized straightaway that the ROA would remain a paper army, good for nothing but anti-Soviet propaganda (though in fact it was mobilized in the final months, when the war was already lost). Silent and impenetrable behind his great melancholy spectacles, Vlasov personified all the sadness of the soldier's life – the empty barracks on Sunday and home so far away. He was intelligent and very quick to see that he had fallen into a trap with no way out. If he continued to play his part nevertheless, he did so, I believe, with the neutral tenacity of the military man, who stays at his post and marches in line even when all is lost.

'Even as he was rallying his men in the prison camps, urging them to enlist at the Germans' side, telling them that only a Russian army could beat Stalin's Russians, Himmler was publicly describing him as "a swine" and only consented to receive him on 20 July, when the Russian general had proved his loyalty by staying with Hitler after many German generals had abandoned him. Vlasov officially founded the KONR, the Committee for the Liberation of the Russian Peoples, in Prague, as late as 14 November 1944; he tried to save face by not mentioning "national socialism" and its racist theories in the KONR's founding document, and declaring his acceptance of German help on condition that it was "compatible with the honour and independence of our homeland".

'I used to see him every day, his face pallid and bespectacled like an intellectual' – reading this description, I thought that Krasnov would probably have said Vlasov didn't know how to ride a horse properly – 'and in his eyes, which avoided mine, I could see the consciousness of the void. He was almost always wearing a uniform with no stripes or stars, because he had

Inferences from a Sabre

vowed not to wear full dress until his country was free and independent again. I was there at his side to deceive him, playing my own little part in that big lie, and he knew it, but he tried to hide this knowledge and to lighten my load of dishonour. I still have a photograph which seems to me the most disturbing image of that infamy and humiliation which implicated all of us; taken in Prague in 1944 – our Nazi-occupied Prague – it shows Vlasov reviewing a German guard of honour in the Hradschin, and responding by raising his arm in the Nazi salute. This photograph is an image of a bottomless humiliation, but I understood from Vlasov's tranquil fleeting gaze, which never met my own – not even at our meetings, at the office of the high command – that of the two of us, I was the infamous one, the traitor, and therefore also the one betrayed, because it was my honour as a soldier which was sullied and humiliated by the false and faithless part that I was compelled to act out to his detriment.

'It was one of the last days in April when I flew with Vlasov to Campoformido. Defeat was already imminent, and the two generals needed to agree plans for regrouping their forces in Austria. The little aeroplane landed in the airfield near Udine. It was late afternoon, damp and sad; Vlasov, in his cloak and without insignias, looked intently at the plain, at the mountains which were already merging with the evening, at the tree-tops stirring slightly in the wind, with the quiet air of someone who has already taken leave of this world. Krasnov had come in his old Fiat, which he had some difficulty, in his wide uniform, climbing out of. Their exchange was brief, a series of very precise details which converged into a very vague and dubious overall plan. They discussed where to rendezvous with their troops; and when Krasnov waxed rhetorical about his great projects – offensives against the Red Army, pincer manoeuvres, and so forth – Vlasov held his peace and smoked one cigarette after another. They could barely tolerate each other's company, and not even their common tragedy or the imminence of the end could bring them closer, perhaps because, until the very last, life is stronger than death and death is powerless over us – even over our dislikes or eccentricities.'

I often reread this letter from von Wojka and imagine the two captains of escape: one grey-clad, the other colourful, one silent, the other talkative, one disillusioned, the other dogmatic. I don't know which is more tragic – the one who sees his own inconsistency clearly or the one who doesn't realize it and so deepens it. In Vlasov's face, Krasnov could have read a truth which he had always refused to accept, and which had once come in a flash to the character Sablin, in his own most famous novel: 'Everything is a lie, the regiment and the colours, military service and Russia, everything is

Inferences from a Sabre

infinitely sad. There is nothing but rain and mud.' Perhaps, after devoting his whole life to forgetting Sablin's immemorial thought, Krasnov saw it now in Vlasov's face and drove it back again with deaf fury.

After that meeting their separate ways led, after many digressions, short-cuts and vicious circles, to the gallows. Krasnov, as we know, arrived there in due course; Vlasov only after a much longer march, which involved his arrest by the Soviets in Bohemia on 12 May. He was hanged in Moscow on 22 August 1946. With an indifference which is eloquent in its dignity, he seems to have waived a possible opportunity of escape that the Americans suggested; when the Russian colonel reponsible for Vlasov invited him to ratify the surrender of the KONR, he replied that he could not do so, because the KONR no longer existed.

The final news or rumours about Krasnov, on the other hand, describe him as speaking confidently in the name of an entire army, even to his jailers in the Lubianka, as if he could still have given orders. I admire and envy his courage and, should someone tell me that it shows stupidity as well, it certainly won't be me, from these comfortable lodgings in a rest-home for the clergy, who moves the Almighty to anger with rash and presumptuous judgements on someone who found himself in the cells of the Lubianka. I merely wonder sometimes whether, during that discussion with Vlasov a few days before their downfall, Krasnov really had no intuition that he too, like the other man, would soon have to strip himself of stars and epaulettes, remove the insignias of his specious glory and, after wearing so many colours, die in grey, as the fallen soldier of Val di Gorto.

I understand, and I share, the obstinacy of anyone who persists in identifying the unknown and nameless man buried and dug up at Villa Santina as Krasnov. And this mistaken hypothesis does contain a truth about his life; for all his pathetic and culpable vanity, there was a streak of humanity in him which deserved that authentic end: deserved the nakedness and absoluteness of death after all the pompous deceit and self-deceit – the salvation of shedding his symbols of command and vanishing into the anonymous crowd of fugitives, a brother among brothers, a son of Eve who returns to the earth and yields up his sabre, with which he has done evil, to her. Perhaps it is this unconscious desire for Krasnov's redemption which has persuaded so many careful, punctilious scholars – and now and then persuades me too – to suppose that this man, who believed in adventure, was capable of admitting, *in extremis*, that his own adventure had been mistaken and that the true, hazardous adventure lay in acknowledging the impossibility of his absurd egocentric dreams, humbly accepting this necessary disappointment, get-

Inferences from a Sabre

ting down from his gaudy horse and walking on the ways of this earth, which welcomes and sustains travellers with no distinction between ranks.

That broken sabre, that bladeless hilt surfacing from the broken grave, brings to mind a sight I haven't seen for years now, not since my legs became too weak to take me up into the woods on Monte Nevoso, where the old eastern border of Italy once ran, and where the boundary now lies between Slovenia and Croatia. If you climb up through the trees towards a hollow called Tri Kaliči, beneath the summit, at a certain point you will reach – or used to reach, but it's sure to be there still – the trunk of a felled tree; the tree had been dead a long time and was already withered and decayed into the ground, though not completely. I climbed up to Tri Kaliči many times, year after year, and that tree was always there, every year more decomposed and closer to dissolving into the earth, but still itself, with its own form, or the memory of its form. As I passed by, I would greet it like a brother and, watching it unmake itself while preserving its individuality, I could accept its fate – feeling it was my fate too, which every passing year brings closer – without fear, almost reverently, affectionately. For there seemed a reassuring tenderness in the earth's embrace, something warm and maternal, similar to how I imagine a woman's love – which priests are denied – the trusting clasp of a sweet, strong body.

The hilt which surfaced from the clods of earth reminds me of this tree-trunk, which will be even more obliterated by now, but still not entirely; it reminds me of the brevity of our life but also of its endurance, and it seems to encourage the great yes which we say to our own eclipse, accepting it serenely, with the bit of resistance which we rightly put up even when we believe, as I do believe, that we are sated and weary of life, because one more afternoon in the Caffè San Marco is a little thing beside eternity but it is something all the same, and perhaps not so very little. And whoever once gripped that hilt, lost and then rediscovered by a grave-digger's shovel, it seems to me that it has been offered by that unknown man as though in sacrifice, not just for himself but for the others too, somehow for you as well and for me, your old Father Guido, who thanks and salutes you now, dear Father Mario, with the same affection as always, with a serene and, I don't know why, a particularly happy soul this morning, grateful I would even say to be looking at the world outside my window.

*

Inferences from a Sabre

No story, say the flax flowers in Andersen's fairy tale, ever ends, and this story too has had its little sequel in reality. Several Cossacks, some of whom have since become my friends, protested to the writer that he, sitting peacefully at his little table, should presume to interpret and explain to them a tragedy which they lived on their own skin; a former partisan, Ateo Borga, wrote an article defending the authenticity of the mythical, historically untenable version of Krasnov's death in Carnia...

Claudio Magris

Map

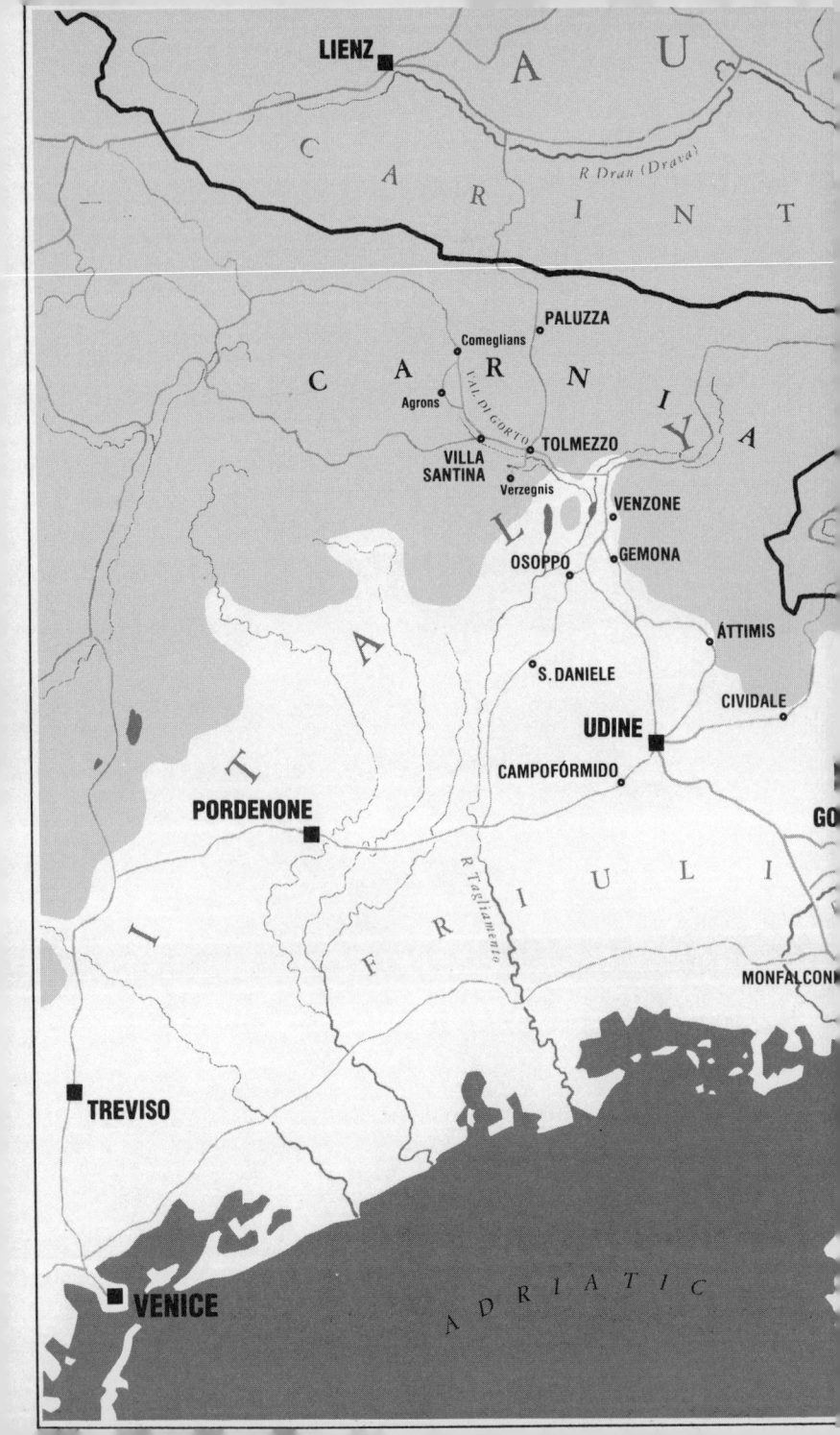

LIENZ

CARINT[HIA]

R Dran (Drava)

PALUZZA

CARNIA

Comeglians

VAL DI GORTO

Agrons

TOLMEZZO

VILLA SANTINA

Verzegnis

VENZONE

GEMONA

OSOPPO

ÁTTIMIS

S. DANIELE

CIVIDALE

UDINE

CAMPOFÓRMIDO

PORDENONE

GO[RIZIA]

R Tagliamento

FRIULI

ITALIA

MONFALCON[E]

TREVISO

VENICE

ADRIATIC